WOOF'S
BAD DAY

by Danae Dobson
Illustrated by Dee deRosa

WORD PUBLISHING
Dallas · London · Sydney · Singapore

This story is dedicated to Clarke Chiasson,
who has been an inspiration to me in many ways.
I admire his loyalty, ambition and qualities of leadership,
but especially his sensitive and caring heart.
I am thankful for the special friendship we share.

Woof's Bad Day

Copyright ©1989 by Danae Dobson for the text. Copyright ©1989 by Dee deRosa for the illustrations. All rights reserved. No portion of this book may be reproduced in any form without the written permission of the publishers, except for brief quotations in reviews.

Scripture quotations are from the King James Version of the Bible and from The Holy Bible, New International Version (NIV). Copyright 1973, 1978, 1984 International Bible Society. Used by permission of Zondervan Bible Publishers.

Library of Congress Cataloging-in-Publication Data

Dobson, Danae.
  Woof's bad day / by Danae Dobson; illustrated by Dee deRosa.
    p.   cm.
  Summary: Through their dog Woof's series of mishaps at a campsite, Mark and Krissy meet the Fosters and are able to tell them about God.
    ISBN 0-8499-8350-9
  [1. Dogs — Fiction. 2. Camping — Fiction. 3. Christian life — Fiction.] I. DeRosa, Dee, ill. II. Title.
PZ7.D6614Wv 1989
[E] — dc20   89-22541
                                                                                                                         CIP
                                                                                                                          AC

Printed in the United States of America
9801239KRU987654321

A MESSAGE FROM
Dr. James Dobson

Before you read about this dog named Woof perhaps you would like to know how these books came to be written. When my children, Danae and Ryan, were young, I often told them stories at bedtime. Many of those tales were about pet animals who were loved by people like those in our own family. Later, I created more stories while driving the children to school in our car pool. The kids began to fall in love with these pets, even though they existed only in our minds. I found out just how much they loved these animals when I made the mistake of telling them a story in which one of their favorite pets died. There were so many tears I had to bring him back to life!

These tales made a special impression on Danae. At the age of twelve, she decided to write her own book about her favorite animal, Woof, and see if Word Publishers would like to print it. She did, and they did, and in the process she became the youngest author in Word's history. Now, ten years later, Danae has written five more, totally new adventures with Woof and the Petersons. And she is still Word's youngest author!

Danae has discovered a talent God has given her, and it all started with our family spending time together, talking about a dog and the two children who loved him. We hope that not only will you enjoy Woof's adventures but that you and your family will enjoy the time spent reading them together. Perhaps you also will discover a talent God has given you.

A warm breeze blew through the open windows of the Petersons' station wagon as it glided down the highway.

"Are we almost there, Dad?" asked the boy in the back seat.

"Not yet, Mark," answered his father, turning down the radio. "But there should be a road sign coming up soon."

After a few miles the Petersons could see an old wooden sign that read: "BIG PINE RECREATIONAL CAMPGROUND." The white arrow pointed toward the south turnoff.

"Oh boy!" exclaimed ten-year-old Krissy, closing the book she'd been reading. "I can hardly wait to see what it looks like!"

The two Peterson children kept close watch as their car turned off the highway and headed up the mountain trail. They had looked forward to this weekend trip for a long time, and now the fun was about to begin!

A sleepy dog in the back lifted his head to look around. His crooked ear flopped over one eye as he took in the view, stopping for a few seconds to yawn.

"Wake up, Woof," said Mark, seeing his furry friend was not his usual perky self. "This is no time to sleep. We have a big day ahead of us."

Woof lay back down in the seat and sniffed at the picnic basket beside him. The smell of salami sandwiches held his attention for the time being. Woof was a very good dog, but he was greedy when it came to food. He loved to eat . . . almost anything!

In a short while the Petersons' station
wagon pulled into the entrance of the campground.

"We're here!" shouted six-year-old Mark, opening the car door excitedly.

"Don't go too far," cautioned Mother as the two children dashed down
the dirt road with Woof behind them.

Mark and Krissy stopped and looked at the beautiful scenery. Tall pine
trees surrounded the campground, and the morning sun shone brightly
on a nearby lake. Some campers were there fishing while others sat near
their tents.

After a few minutes Mark and Krissy went back to help set up camp, while Woof trotted into the forest to explore. The fresh scent of pine needles and other strange smells tempted him to wander farther and farther away. But he wasn't worried. He would follow his own scent back to the campground.

As Woof was wandering among the trees, something caught his eye. A tiny head about the size of a golf ball poked out of a dead log. Woof didn't know the creature was a chipmunk, but he found it fascinating! He walked closer to get a better look. The little animal seemed just as curious as Woof. He stared out of the log with his pink nose wiggling rapidly.

Suddenly the chipmunk ducked back into the log. Woof peered into the opening, wondering why his little friend had disappeared so fast. He soon learned the reason why.

"Ggrooooowwlll!" echoed a mighty roar that shook the forest. Woof wheeled around to see a large bear towering over him. The bear stared angrily as he stood on his hind feet, saliva dripping from his fangs.

Woof's heart jumped into his throat! He ran back toward the camp as fast as he could go. The angry bear was right behind him. Fortunately Woof could run very fast, even with a crooked leg. He dodged around trees and through the thicket until finally the bear was thrown off the trail.

The Peterson family was taken by surprise when Woof came tearing back into the campground. He dived for the tent and sat trembling in the corner.

"What happened to *you*?" asked Krissy as she opened the flap that served as a door.

"Woof looks as though he's seen a ghost," laughed Mark, peering inside the tent. "Come on, boy. Let's go have some *real* fun!"

Woof crawled out of the tent and meekly followed Mark and Mr. Peterson down to the lake. He was still frightened, but he felt safe now that he was with the family. He wished he could make them understand what had happened, but there just wasn't any way to tell them.

While Mark and Father fished at the lake, Krissy and Mother prepared the lunch they had packed in the picnic basket. They wondered why one of the sandwiches was missing, but it wasn't too long before they figured out who was to blame.

"Why, that sneaky little dog!" exclaimed Mother. "Doesn't he ever get enough to eat?"

"I don't think so," laughed Krissy. "But one of these days his appetite is going to get him into trouble."

Back at the lake Mark and his dad had caught five fish. Woof was having a wonderful time splashing in the water. He was also trying to catch some fish, but Mark made him stay far away so he wouldn't scare off the trout.

Woof had finally forgotten about the bear as he jumped in and out of the water. He was having so much fun he almost didn't notice the strange-looking animal that was watching him from behind a bush. Woof walked to the shore and shook himself to dry off his fur. He spotted the odd-looking creature again and ran to make a new friend.

It was the ugliest animal he had ever seen—a round ball with points all over its fur. Woof sniffed at him curiously. He had never seen a porcupine before. The porcupine did not appreciate Woof's company at all and tried to wobble away from the annoying dog. But Woof continued to run around him, barking playfully and nipping at his tail.

Mark heard his dog barking and came out of the water to check on him. Seeing the porcupine, Mark dropped his fishing pole and yelled, "Get back, Woof!" But it was too late. Poor Woof had sharp quills sticking in his face, nose and ears!

He yelped in misery as they carried him back to the campsite. Woof was really having a bad day, all right!

"What happened?" asked Krissy when she saw Woof's condition.

"He had a little disagreement with a porcupine," answered Mr. Peterson. "We have to get these spines out quick!"

Mother wasted no time in taking out her first aid kit and going to work. She gently pulled out every quill and put medicine on the wounds. By the time she finished, Woof felt a lot better. He watched the family as they ate lunch and talked about the fish they had caught.

When they were through eating, Mark and Krissy asked their father if they could go on a hike.

"Yes, if you don't mind me going with you," he replied. "There are bears around the campground, and they could be dangerous."

Woof thought to himself, "I know! I know!"

With that, the two children put on their jeans and hiking boots and filled their canteens with water.

"Stay here, Woof," instructed Mark, as he patted his dog on the head.

"And stay out of trouble!" added Krissy.

Woof watched as the three headed off on their adventure. Ordinarily he would have wanted to go with them, but he had had enough excitement for one day. Besides, he thought that bear might be waiting for him out there somewhere.

As Woof lay on his blanket near the tent, a wonderful scent drifted into his nostrils. "FOOD!" he thought.

Quickly he glanced over to see what Mrs. Peterson was doing. She was in a lawn chair reading a book. Should he find out where the great smell was coming from? Why not? He followed the scent over a little hill and down to a row of picnic tables. There were people sitting at the tables who had just enjoyed a good old-fashioned barbecue. The food smelled so good it made Woof's mouth water. More than anything else, he wanted to bite into that sweet-smelling meat.

As Woof was wondering how he could get some of the scraps, the people decided to leave. He couldn't believe his eyes! They threw all the plates into a huge trash can nearby. Woof waited patiently for the campers to pack their things, his mouth watering as he stood in the shadows. He was going to have the greatest meal of his life!

Finally he had the garbage to himself. He quickly turned over the can, spilling the contents all over the ground. It was too good to be true! Woof began gobbling the meat and chewing the bones as though he were starving.

He ate and ate—long after he was full. It was wonderful. Dogs don't usually smile, but Woof was actually grinning with joy while he feasted. But after a while, he started to feel miserable. His stomach began to hurt, and he became a little dizzy. He finally collapsed by the empty trash can, unable to move a muscle.

When Mr. Peterson and the children returned from their hike, they immediately noticed their dog was missing.

"Where's Woof?" asked Krissy nervously.

Mrs. Peterson looked up from her book. "I'm not sure," she said. "I thought he was here with me."

Just then, a middle-aged man in a plaid shirt walked up to the Petersons. "Do you own a dog?" he asked.

"Yes, and he's missing," answered Father. "Have you seen him?"

"I believe so, and I think he's sick. He's lying on the ground as if he's paralyzed."

"Let's go," said Mr. Peterson.

Krissy, Mark and their parents followed the man to the picnic area. "Oh my!" said Mother as she put her hands over her mouth.

Woof had indeed gotten himself in a mess this time. He lay flat on his back, his round belly twice its normal size. His four legs stuck straight up in the air stiffly. Although Woof couldn't move, he rolled his big brown eyes toward his family when they walked toward him. Just a few splinters of dry bones lay on the ground near his head. That was all that remained from his feast.

Mark and Krissy tried not to laugh as they lifted their dog and carried him back to the tent.

"You've really done it this time, Woof," said Mark as he struggled to carry the overfed animal. "I hope you've learned your lesson."

"You are a glutton, Woof!" Krissy added. "You should be ashamed of yourself!"

Woof did feel very foolish. But whenever he thought of all those ribs and the fat and meat, he smiled again.

For the rest of the afternoon, Woof stayed on his blanket near the tent. He was still too full to move, so he drifted off to sleep.

Mark and Krissy spent their time playing Frisbee and horseshoes, but it wasn't as much fun without Woof.

As the sun started to set around the campground, Father began to build a small fire.

"Is dinner going to be ready soon?" asked Mark. "I'm starved."

"Yes," answered Mother. "We're going to fry the fish you and Dad caught this afternoon."

"I don't think Woof is going to find the food very tempting," joked Krissy.

Woof looked over and wagged his tail a little bit. He was feeling better, but he still felt like he weighed 300 pounds.

All was peaceful around the campground as the Petersons thanked God for the food and enjoyed their meal by the fire. In the distance there were flickers of light where other campers had built small fires, too.

Just as Mark was reaching for the marshmallows, a young boy walked up toward their camp. "Hello," he said as he approached the Peterson family. "I'm Jason Foster. My dad was the one who told you about your dog this afternoon."

"Oh, yes," replied Mother. "We were just getting ready to roast marshmallows. Why don't you join us?"

"Well, all right," Jason said as he took a seat next to Mark. "I came by to see how your dog is feeling. He seemed to be in bad shape this afternoon."

"Woof *was* in bad shape all right," agreed Krissy. "But he seems to be doing better now. Let's just say he's overloaded for the time being."

The Petersons laughed as they looked back at their homely, overstuffed dog. Woof opened one eye and lifted his crooked ear, but he was too exhausted and full to respond. Even the wonderful smell of marshmallows didn't tempt him to move. Ordinarily, Woof would have been begging for a few bites. But this time the thought of food didn't interest him. He only wanted to sleep and get over his afternoon feast.

For the rest of the night, the Peterson children sang by the fire and talked with their new friend. They were having so much fun they barely noticed it was close to nine o'clock.

"Mark, Krissy, it's time for bed," reminded Mother.

"I'd best be going anyway," Jason said, as he stood up and dusted off his jeans. "My dad is waiting for me."

"Thanks for stopping by," said Mark. "Maybe we'll see you tomorrow."

"Wait a minute," said Krissy. "Since tomorrow's Sunday, we're going to have a church service in the morning. Would you like to come?"

"I don't know," replied Jason nervously. "I've never been to church before."

"It won't be a regular church service," said Krissy. "We're just going to have devotions out here on the mountain. How about it?"

"Well, I'll have to ask my dad," Jason answered.

"Be here at ten o'clock in the morning if you can come," said Mr. Peterson.

"We'll see," replied Jason. With that, he headed into the night.

Within minutes Mark and Krissy had snuggled into their sleeping bags and zipped them up all the way.

"I've had so much fun today!" exclaimed Krissy, as she fluffed up her pillow.

"Me too," agreed Mark. "Even with all of Woof's mischief!"

"Shhhh," whispered Mother from the other side of the tent. "It's time to go to sleep."

The campfire slowly smoldered and turned to ashes as the Petersons fell asleep under the stars.

When morning came, the family was awakened by birds singing in the trees. Woof was already up and looking forward to breakfast. Mark found him by the lake trying to catch a fish. His stomach was still oversized, but his energy had returned.

"Woof! Here boy," called Mark. Woof was soaking wet as he bounded across the shore in the direction of his friend.

"Come on," Mark laughed. "Let's go back to camp."

When they returned, Mother was frying eggs and sausage in a skillet over the fire. Woof licked his chops as he smelled the appetizing food.

"No, no," scolded Krissy. "You stay away from our breakfast." Woof looked disappointed as he sat down on his blanket.

As the Petersons finished eating, they looked up to see Jason and his father coming toward them.

Mr. Peterson stood up and shook hands with Jason's father. "I'm glad you could join us," he said warmly.

"I'm not into religion very much," Mr. Foster commented. "But you are such nice folks that I want to hear what you have to say."

Everyone sat in a circle as Father opened the Bible and began to read from the Gospel of John. "For God so loved the world, that he gave his only begotten Son, that whosoever believeth in Him should not perish, but have everlasting life."

"What does that mean?" asked Mr. Foster.

Father explained how Jesus came to take away man's sin by dying on the cross and how He loves each person as though he were the only one on earth.

Jason and Mr. Foster asked lots of questions, and Mr. Peterson answered them by reading from the Bible. They closed their devotions with a prayer, thanking God for His blessings.

As they finished, Krissy turned to Jason and smiled. "I want you to have this," she said as she handed him her Bible.

"Thank you," Jason said gratefully. "I've never read the Bible before, but I sure will now."

"That's nice of you," said Mr. Foster. "I would like to read it too."

"I have one last, special verse just for Woof," Mr. Peterson laughed. Bending down and looking straight into Woof's big brown eyes, Father quoted from Haggai 1:6 "…you eat, but never have enough…"

Woof didn't know why everyone was laughing at him. All he knew was that it was time to eat and he was hungry. But he wasn't interested in the doggie crunchies that lay in his bowl. He had his mind on something better!

While the Peterson family loaded the station wagon and said good-bye to the Fosters, Woof trotted down to the lake. He was *determined* to catch a fish before it was time to go home. He splashed around in the water, looking beneath the surface for any kind of movement.

In a few moments Woof became very excited. A small dark shadow passed beneath him in the water. But before he could turn to catch it, the creature rose to the surface. It was not a fish but a snapping turtle! It quickly lunged for Woof's tail, which was wagging just above the water, and clamped down tightly with its powerful jaws.

Woof howled with surprise! He twisted and turned in the water, but the turtle hung on. Woof ran up the road as fast as he could go—with the turtle bouncing along behind.

"Oh no, Dad," said Mark. "Woof is in trouble again!"

Mr. Peterson called the dog to him and quickly pried the turtle's jaws off his tail.

"We better get Woof in the car before he gets himself killed," laughed Krissy.

Everyone waved good-bye as the station wagon rattled down the dusty mountain trail.

"Well, at least one good thing came from Woof's gluttony," Mother commented.

"What's that?" asked Mark.

"We never would have met Jason or his dad if it hadn't been for Woof's mischief. But because of it, we got to know them, and they came to know about Jesus."

"That's true," agreed Krissy, patting her dog on the head. "Isn't it exciting?"

As the Peterson family laughed and talked about the trip, Woof poked his head out the rear window and felt the soft breeze against his face. He had learned some valuable lessons this weekend, lessons he would not soon forget. As he was thinking of his misfortune, a familiar scent interrupted his thoughts. Woof sniffed the air and suddenly became excited as he leaned further out the window.

Just then, the Petersons' car drove past a sign that read: "ARNOLD'S RIB JOINT — 1/2 mile ahead." Woof's tail was wagging happily.